The Border

&

A Young Man in the Know

by RÉGIS DEBRAY

Translated by Helen R. Lane

Grove Press, Inc., New York

The Border

"Maybe this time it'll be for me," Mauro said aloud in a drawl to mock his hope.

The car slowed down, went by him slowly, and speeded up again. He shrugged his shoulders, lowered his hand, and waited for the next car. Not ten seconds later he heard the squeal of tires behind him. He turned around: the car had stopped on the cement shoulder a hundred yards farther down the road. An old, dark purple Chrysler. Mauro didn't budge. "They won't fool me this time," he thought, determined not to make a move for nothing.

In the two hours since the driver of a candy truck had let him out in front of the cafeteria he was headed for to deliver jaw-breakers and chocolate bars, he had already been taken in once: a car had slowed down as it came by, he had slung his canvas bag over his shoulder, begun to run, and come to a sudden halt ten yards farther on, feeling sheepish. It was only someone who was braking to enter the motel whose heart-shaped turquoise swimming pool he saw gleaming a few yards off the road, or someone who was stopping to have something to drink at the cafeteria. People probably didn't stop often at this cafeteria that was too far from the road, badly advertised, and shabby looking with its peeling façade—alongside the gleaming motels all along the road that called attention to themselves with lots of signs, neon arrows, and Gothic fronts. Mauro was just wondering whether he had been right to take this road, Route 17, that runs along the East Coast instead of going inland and taking 301, the big highway running north and south, which was much more heavily traveled, and wondering whether he wouldn't be forced to take a Greyhound to get to 301, at Allendale or Statesboro, a little farther down in Georgia. He was even beginning to wonder if he would ever hitchhike his way out of South Carolina. It was a good spot though, just after the last curve as you leave Jacksonboro, one that cars come out of at reduced speed. After that comes a long, straight stretch of road.

No one got out of the Chrysler. Nobody blew the horn. All Mauro saw was heads looking at him out the back window, but since he had the sun in his eyes he couldn't make out what their faces looked like. Someone knocked against the glass door of the cafeteria. He turned his head. It was the waitress, a little blonde, motioning with her hand for him to come over. She said something to him from behind the glass, but he couldn't make out what it was. Then she smiled at him to make him feel confident again. Even though not many people stopped at the place, she was gotten up like a real barmaid in Times Square, quite clean and pretty, with a paper cap over her hair, a pleated skirt, and a spotless blouse. She had looked so happy to finally have somebody in the place when he stayed on to have a hamburger and a cup of coffee with cream, after the driver of the candy truck had left. They had talked a lot, she had shown an interest in his lot in life, and since then she had come out to the edge of the highway three times to give him a few very timid words of encouragement.

Mauro smiled back at her to reassure her. When the car began to honk and someone called something out of its door, he finally made up his mind. He slung his bag over his shoulder, and with his head bent over to one side he ran toward the car. The girl waved good-by to him from behind her glass door. It was a tense smile, as if she didn't know whether she was glad or sad to see him leave. She stood on tiptoe so as not to lose sight of him. "Too bad," Mauro thought as he ran along the road. "We were beginning to like each other a whole lot," and he waved back at her with his free hand.

He was out of breath when he reached the car. Disappointment. The rear license plate said "South Carolina." That meant that these were local people who wouldn't be going very far. The front door of the car opened and a blond guy, quite young, who was sitting next to the driver, put his foot on the ground. Mauro immediately began to tell them that if they weren't leaving the state there was no use in their taking him, but the other guy interrupted him:

"We're going to Georgia. Savannah. Does that suit you?"

"Great. That's where I'm headed," Mauro replied.

"Get in the back then."

Savannah was sixty miles away, on the other side of the Savannah River, the first big town in Georgia. "Once there it'll be easy to take off again," he said to himself.

Mauro opened the door, put his bag down on the floor, and flopped down onto the back seat. The car started up again smoothly. There were four of them including him in the car. The man at the wheel hadn't opened his mouth. He tried to thank him, but the man didn't even turn around, so he shut up. The driver was the oldest of the three, about forty, tanned, unshaven, with greasy hair that hadn't been cut in a long time, and dandruff on his shoulders. He had large hands that were hairy on top with black fingernails, and he was chewing a cigar butt. The little guy in the back next to Mauro looked much younger, barely twenty, with short-cropped brown hair, sitting there impassively with his arms crossed. He was wearing a dirty T-shirt, beige cotton pants, and tennis shoes. The serious way he crossed his short little arms that swelled with biceps as big as your hand and the way he looked straight in front of him was really rather funny; he was too deliberate, too tense. The sturdy blond with whom he had spoken before he got in was in the front. He had a paper cup in his hand. Mauro leaned over and saw bottles of Coca-Cola and a little half-empty bottle of whisky on the floor in front of him. When he had looked carefully at the three not very clean, unshaven men, Mauro thought: "These guys at least haven't got piles of money."

The car was going quite fast. They seemed to be in a hurry to get where they were going. No belongings in the car, no suitcases, no bags. No one said anything to him or looked at him. They didn't talk among themselves either. This tense silence, like a veiled hostility, made Mauro feel ill at ease. It lasted a good half-hour. Mauro couldn't stand it any longer. "So you're from Jacksonboro," he finally blurted out, point-blank, just to be saying something.

"No, not Jacksonboro. From around there," the blond replied.

"And you're going to Savannah on business?"

"Yes, on business."

After a silence the blond asked: "You're not from the South, are you? You can tell just from listening to you."

"No. This is the first time I've been down here," Mauro said.

"Where you from?"

"New York."

"Just as I thought!" the driver murmured, as if he were talking to himself. These were the first words he had spoken.

"I'm from New York, but I haven't been there for a long time," Mauro then explained. "I'm really from Palermo, in Italy."

The little guy next to him turned his eyes toward him and repeated: "In Italy?"

"Yes, in Europe, if you prefer," Mauro said.

"You speak good English," the blond said.

"I've been in the States two years."

The driver looked at him in turn in the rear-view mirror and said: "You look hefty for an Italian."

"Thanks," Mauro said with a smile. "But the Italians wouldn't thank you."

"Do you always hitchhike?" the blond asked.

"Yeah, all the time. It isn't so hard with all the tourists stopping."

"You'd have better luck on 301, you know. The tourists all go that way."

"I know," Mauro said. "But I came across a guy who was going to Charleston, so I went with him. That's why I left 301."

"Did you sleep in Charleston last night?"

"Yes, a little ways outside, on the outskirts of town. Near the tobacco factory."

"The niggers didn't bother you? There's lots of them around here, you know?"

"No, why should they?" Mauro replied and laughed.

"You never know what can happen to a white man running around alone in South Carolina," the blond went on in a harsh voice.

He snickered, thumped the driver lightly on the back, and the driver agreed with a little sniffle, shook his head, and looked at Mauro pityingly. Since Mauro didn't answer he went on:

"You have to be born here to understand that." He gave Mauro a friendly little tap on the arm.

"Come on, don't let it bother you," he said, changing his tone of voice. "Have some Coke."

Mauro was happy. The blond was definitely the most likable. You could at least talk to him. He had a surprisingly tanned face for a man who was certainly not more than thirty, and looked even tanner because of his sunbleached hair. He had on a grease-stained cotton sports shirt, and his arms were tanned only as far as the elbows. It was obvious that he came from the country.

"Give him some whisky along with it," the driver said.

"Thank you very much. My name is Mauro," he answered without transition.

"O.k., Mauro, I'm Dan," the blond said, and passed him the paper cup with half-melted crushed ice floating in it.

He had poured out a good stiff drink of whisky.

"Steve," the little guy with brown hair next to him blurted, still scornful and sullen.

Mauro instinctively turned toward the driver, but the man didn't say a word. The silence lasted a good minute. "Not very polite," Mauro said to himself, "really not very polite. He didn't need to pick me up, after all, if I was going to be a bother to him."

It was Dan who broke the silence. "He's George," he said, pointing to him with his thumb.

George looked at Dan out of the corner of his eye, shrugged his shoulders, and grumbled something incomprehensible. He spit the stump of his dead cigar out the window, swerved violently to the left to pass an old broken-down car that was backfiring in the middle of the road, and the car raced on, still accelerating. In the distance layers of white fog trembled above the road, which was surprisingly deserted for the month of June. It was not countryside around here, but the eternal artificial décor that endlessly bordered the road: billboards, motels, service stations, white wooden bungalows, as if the road left one cluster of buildings only to fall into another immediately afterward.

They had driven for a good hour when Mauro said: "We must not be far from Hardeeville now."

"We're real close," Steve said with a stiff smile.

"Yes, real close, real close," George repeated in an absent-minded, preoccupied voice. "Hardeeville is just before the Savannah River and the suspension bridge, just before we get to Georgia."

Bent over the wheel, George watched the road. The two others also seemed to be watching. Just after a curve in the road, as he was picking up speed again, George suddenly slowed down and got into the left lane. Two policemen stationed after the curve on their motorcycles, with their high-visored caps on backward, were nonchalantly watching the cars go by. The sun made the chrome of the fenders of the motorcycles and the edges of their smoked-glass windshields gleam.

"I was at the right speed, huh, you guys?" George said, having suddenly become motionless and forcing himself not to look at the cops.

"Stay that way," Dan said reassuringly. "Sixty miles an hour—that's perfect. Don't worry."

Dan's tic had gotten twice as bad: his mouth twitched all the time. Each time it twitched it made a little hollow in the corner of his mouth, big enough to put your finger in. At the same time he turned his head imperceptibly to one side and his eye blinked.

The line of cars ahead of them had grown thicker, so that they had to slow down even more. A bottleneck had formed. Since they were in the second lane, along the center line, the cops barely saw them as they went by almost at a crawl.

The traffic thinned out shortly afterward. George picked up speed again, but much less than before. Cars passed them several times. "They can't afford a ticket," Mauro said to himself, impressed. "Speed limits must be no joke around here."

"It'd be stupid to take a risk on account of the car anyhow," Steve said brusquely, breaking the silence. "Don't you think so, Mr. Spott?"

"When you come right down to it, you may be right, son," George replied. "You have to do things right in life. What do you think, Dan?"

"There's still time to go to Richard's," Dan said. "He can do something about the car."

"I thought of that, Dan, but I was afraid on account of the time it'd take. And then I didn't want to bother him about it . . ."

"I think we can trust Richard, Mr. Spott."

"That's not the question, son. The question is, if the lieutenant got the lead out of his pants . . ."

"Well, he's certainly not going to go to all the farmers in the association," Dan interrupted. "You can see that from here . . ."

"Yes, you're right. We can always go see," George concluded. "We'll turn at Gatinburg."

Then Mauro said: "If you have somebody to see,

never mind about me. As long as you let me off on the highway I can always find another car."

There was a general outcry. "Of course not, you're staying with us," George said. "If it doesn't bother you, we won't be very long. In any case we'll be in Savannah before tonight."

"Now that we're pals we can't leave each other just like that," Dan blurted, laughing.

"Are people where you come from in such a hurry they can't take time out for a ride?" Steve said, going Dan one better.

"Oh, no, I have plenty of time," Mauro replied. He didn't know what to say to apologize. He was ashamed of having wanted to drop them for so selfish a reason as continuing on his own. They already considered him one of them, and he'd gone and treated them like a bus passenger treats the driver!

"Whatever you say," he said. "I'd like nothing better than to go with you. I just didn't want to bother you, that's all."

"If you knew how you're bothering us," George said with a disarming smile. It was George himself who had broken the ice! The idea of having pals warmed Mauro's heart. Perhaps they'd spend some time together in Georgia, in Savannah or Atlanta or wherever. He didn't know a soul in the South. But they were at home here. Sometimes it's comforting to be able to tell yourself that in a place that's really a foreign country, after four days of hitchhiking, and three thousand miles from Palermo.

"And you're going a long way this way?" George continued, smiling at him in the rear-view mirror.

"To Miami," Mauro confessed.

The name brought an admiring whistle from Dan and Steve.

"If you hitchhike in the Everglades, be careful not to get caught by an alligator," Dan exclaimed. "Be on the lookout!"

Dan and Steve both burst out laughing at once. Not George. He went on as if he had heard nothing:

"You gonna look for work there?"

"Yes. They tell me it's easiest there."

"That's no lie," George said.

"Do you think I'll find any?" Mauro asked.

"A young guy like you will find all the work you want. Especially this time of year, with all the tourists that are there. They always need somebody in the hotels. All you have to do is walk along Miami Beach and ask at each hotel. You won't have far to go, believe me."

"Haven't the Cubans taken everything?" Steve asked.

"Maybe, but they still would rather hire an Italian than a Cuban," George answered.

"Is it true what they say in the papers about the Cubans?" Mauro ventured. "Are there really that many down there?"

"A whole section of town," George said. "They don't know where to put 'em. They let anybody come in. They don't even need a visa, so you can imagine."

"That must lower wages," Steve said.

"That crazy damned Red with the beard too. . . . What are they waiting for? Why don't they kick him in the ass?" Dan said, and angrily poured a big gulp of whisky down his gullet. "A mechanical jumping jack like that—it shouldn't be hard to make spare parts out of him, right, George?"

"Sure, Dan, sure." George snapped his fingers. "We'd have a go-around if I was there. We'll see if the Reds are going to get as far north as Savannah now! But you'll see. Florida is still a great place," he said, his voice growing softer as he addressed Mauro.

"You ever been to Florida, Mr. Spott?" Steve asked ingenuously.

George inhaled cigarette smoke through his teeth and said: "If they ask you that, you're to say you know nothing about it."

"I didn't mean any harm, Mr. Spott," Steve said in embarrassment. He blinked his eyes and stopped smiling.

"That's lucky for you!" George said. Distracted by the conversation, he had accelerated again. Dan cast worried glances at the speedometer, and then at George, but did not dare make too many remarks aloud. They were coming in to Gatinburg, without the scenery having changed at all: billboards, motels, service stations.

"It'll soon be time to turn," Dan said.

"You'll tell me how to get to Richard's, right?" George said. Steve's remarks had put him in a bad humor again. "Go on and get Mauro something to drink. He's dying of thirst."

"No, really, I don't want any," Mauro answered. "It just makes me sweat more."

"Whatever you say, son. Nobody's forcing you, see? You're in a free country here . . ."

"But you go ahead and have a drink," Mauro said,

remembering his manners. "You need one. You must be tired of driving."

"O.k., Dan, do as he says. Pour me a cupful of rye."

"Do you want ice with it?" Dan asked. "It's water now."

"No, throw the ice away."

And at the first intersection he turned right.

Before Hardeeville, west of Route 17, there was a change of country. The road was narrow, but paved, or at least had been once. It was rough going with the mudholes and the ruts and the puddles of water left standing after a storm. Mauro wondered whether he was not getting lost once again.

Tires had left traces of dried mud on the road. Barbed wire separated one orange grove from another. There were no farms or clusters of buildings anywhere. Then the road began to run through a pine woods;

there were crossroads with wooden signposts that were almost completely worn away. The car went along at a fair speed through this labyrinth of little roads, almost footpaths. At one crossroads they met two men, two whites, who were walking along with their hunting rifles on their shoulders. For a long time they were held up by a 1930 rattletrap ahead of them towing a motorboat on a trailer with half-deflated tires, the road being too narrow to pass. They could smell a pond, but there was nothing to be seen from the road.

"Do they hunt ducks here?" Mauro asked.

"Yes, ducks, rabbits, teal, a little bit of everything." And then with a hearty laugh: "There's things for a white man to hunt around here, right, Dan?"

"You can say that again," Dan agreed, with a smile that bared all his teeth. "You can say that again."

Then the woods thinned out. There were fields of sugar cane on the left, and strange stretches of flat land on the right; after a curve the road widened to a big yard, and the car braked and stopped in front of a group of low, open sheds made of white wood. Three big trucks were parked in the yard. An unused gas pump with a rusted handle stood comically at the edge of the road. Two or three dirty dogs came out from under the trucks and began to bark as the men stepped out of the car. Along the sides of the central building laundry was hung out to dry: striped shirts, faded jeans, overalls, colored shorts. Farther on, a path led to shacks of tarred cardboard and corrugated iron, leaning against each other so as not to fall down: a general store, houses for the hired help, or outhouses. "It's too hot to go and see," Mauro said as he caught sight of the shacks behind the clothes hung out to dry.

"They're loading already!" George exclaimed as he stood in front of the railed trucks with their tailgates down. In front of each truck was a pyramid of watermelons, like bottle-green rugby balls, shining in the sun. There was a chain of Negroes between the watermelons and the tailgates of the trucks.

"I'd like to be at the farm to supervise my loading too," George stormed. This spectacle made him angry; he walked back and forth along the road, examining the trucks, questioning the drivers. Dan. and Steve followed him respectfully.

"Don't worry, Mr. Spott," Steve said.

"That goddamn bastard picked just the right time to get underfoot too!" George went on, muttering between his teeth without having heard a word, his face streaming with sweat.

"Come on, calm down, Mr. Spott," Steve began again.

"Two or three days, I tell you," Dan interrupted. "That's nothing to make a fuss about."

"And who's going to take care of *my* melons? The niggers maybe? Or the preacher? Or the state highway patrol? If I'd known, I wouldn't have picked 'em so soon," George added. "They're going to rot."

"There was no way of knowing beforehand," Steve said.

"Otherwise it wouldn't have been a surprise to the bastard," Dan concluded.

George smiled and went on pacing up and down. Mauro, who had not dared intervene, smiled too because he found it funny, but not really understanding why, just wanting to be in on the conversation.

They had lowered their voices as they exchanged these last remarks, but some of the Negroes must have heard them, for they turned their heads toward them and exchanged a few quick words in a low voice. One of them even dropped a watermelon, breaking the rhythm of the whole chain. Someone out of sight in the back of the truck swore, and the Negroes formed the chain again. George suddenly calmed down for good. The others said no more. They went toward the building with a slightly raised porch bordering the back of the big yard. It was a grocery store, in dirty white wood, with a screen door. Rusty gasoline cans were strewn about beneath the veranda. A red Pepsi-Cola cooler and a big carton filled to the brim with empty beer cans and bottles stood on either side of the door.

Mauro had stayed behind.

"Hey, I can leave if you're going to be here for quite a while," he said, just so that they'd remember he was there.

The other three turned around.

"I can take one of these trucks when it's full and get back on 17," he continued, a bit embarrassed.

"Of course not. We won't be long, Mauro," George growled politely. "Stay with us, old man. Just long enough to see the boss, Richard, a good friend of mine. We have to change cars," he added.

"Is that so?" Mauro said, astonished. "The one we were in wasn't running badly."

"Yes, but there's a garage here. It's best to get it looked over and greased and all. We'll pick it up on our way back. Richard will lend us another one to go on with."

"Whatever you guys say," Mauro said, falling in step with them.

"Would you mind waiting over there?" George said. "We have to arrange it with Richard. We have to talk."

"All right, I'll wait," Mauro said.

"It won't take long," Dan added.

They went on toward the building in back. Reaching the porch, Dan turned around at the door though and yelled to him from the distance: "You hungry or thirsty?"

"Both," Mauro replied.

"O.k., fella. I'll have them make a sandwich for you. Get a beer in the grocery while you're waiting."

Mauro stood there with his arms dangling, his feet in the dust, the sun on his neck. The air was stagnant, with not a breath of air. It burned his lungs, and was made even thicker by the drawling sounds of a radio that seemed to be coming from infinitely far away, and were in fact coming from the grocery store: gospel hymns with an organ and choirs, alternating with old jazz tunes. On the other side of the road the view was cut off by the high green shoots of a field of sugar cane. Farther off in the distance, the pine woods that they had come through on the way could be seen. Mauro breathed in as deeply as he could: no smell of resin, but a stale odor of overheated garbage. It was coming from the farmyard, a little square enclosed with a barbed-wire fence, on the other end of the big yard, not far from the grocery. Mauro drew closer: some little pigs were rooting in the mud with their snouts and swallowing the watermelon rinds strewn over the ground and rolling in the mud. A little boy who was almost an albino, the son of the boss, doubtless, was sitting watching and tickling the pigs with a stick. A cloud of hens and roosters were fighting for food under the pigs' trotters, and he stood there a good five minutes watching them peck at the slices of melon with their beaks, grab one, and go off in a corner to gorge themselves on the juice and the seeds all by themselves. Then Mauro discovered a rather spacious bungalow behind the grocery, with wooden steps and neatly whitewashed walls that clashed with the dingy gray of the other buildings. A combination garden and yard separated the back of the grocery store from the front of the house, with an enormous oak in the middle that made a great circle of shade. Protected from the sun, black women, with young girls among them with colored madras scarves over their hair, were sitting next to each other in the shade of the tree on kitchen chairs placed in a circle, each with a pan between her knees. Each of them in turn leaned down over a big flat basin in the middle, drew out a handful of green beans, put them in her pan, and without looking strung them with absent-minded dexterity. They were apparently speaking to each other in low voices, listlessly, their pans between their knees, exchanging rapid glances, with fixed smiles on their faces, quietly and steadily working their beans over the while. "They're in the shade at least," Mauro said to himself enviously.

One of the two trucks, full now, was already leaving. The motor throbbed, pulled against its load with a creak, and finally took off, its metal panels all trembling, and turned in the yard to go on its way again, raising clouds of dust and sand. Deafened and blinded, Mauro closed his eyes. When he opened them again, the whole team of black loaders—barefoot, in blue jeans, with an undershirt or a worn sports shirt with the tails sticking out—was breaking up. Left to themselves, their colored caps and their enormous sun glasses made them look like tourists. They went off in groups of two or three and hunched down under the remaining truck to have a bit of shade while the others loaded. Others leaned on the fenders of a large green and white carcass of a car with no tires and its axle resting on the ground. The little blond boy was going from one group to the other. They smiled when they caught sight of him and called out to him; his name was Matt. At least that is what the Negroes called him: "Home from school already, Matt?" "Maybe you didn't go, huh?" "Put your stick down, Matt," another shouted, "go get the ball and bats and we'll have a game together, O.k., kid?" And Matt laughed, and came over to play who's-the-strongest with them.

Seeing this, Mauro drew closer. There was immediately a silence and they looked at him scoffingly, their eyes full of arrogance. Mauro did not force himself on them and went off toward some bales of old hay heaped up in a pile, with the thought of stealing into a little shaded hole in the middle and resting. Someone behind him called: "Hey, you, where you from?"

It was a young white man, a fat man with a crew cut dressed in blue work overalls, hailing him from the top of the truck-bed, his hands on his hips.

"I'm a friend of those other guys, the ones who came

in that car over there," Mauro said, pointing to the Chrysler.

"Hey, isn't that George's car?" the other man said, and jumped down from the truck.

"Yes it is. I came with him. Do you know him?"

"Do I know George!" the white man answered with a laugh. "Do you have something to do right now?" he added.

"Yes, I'd like to go sleep," Mauro said.

"O.k." And turning to the men standing in a chain, he said: "Stop a minute, you-all."

They passed the melons back the way they had come, put them back on the pile, and began to break up the chain.

"Did I tell you to clear out altogether?" the white man roared. Stopped cold by his voice, the others took their places again, grumbling and exchanging jokes that Mauro didn't understand because they were in Negro dialect. They laughed among themselves and, profiting from the break, they took off their caps and worked the stiffness out of their arms, and those who had handkerchiefs around their necks wiped their faces gleaming with sweat.

The white man walked over toward Mauro. "Here," he said, "supervise in my place. I want to go shake hands with old George and see what his visit is all about. I'll be back right away," and he put a sort of chronometer in Mauro's hand.

"What am I supposed to do with this?" Mauro asked.

"Every time a watermelon goes in the truck, you push on the button. Then when you're through, you've got the exact number of watermelons you've loaded; it's to simplify selling them."

"It's not complicated," Mauro said.

"No, it isn't," the other said, and went off toward the grocery. The Negroes stared mockingly at Mauro, visibly impatient to get on with the work because of the sun.

"Come on, you guys," Mauro shouted to them, "I'm coming."

He immediately went over to the truck and jumped inside, clutching his counter tightly in his hand. The bed of the truck, covered with a large green canvas, was as cool as a vault. There was a good half of it to fill yet. He found the work very easy. With each watermelon that the last man in the chain threw into the hands of one of the two who were busy arranging the watermelons, one on top of the other, in the truck bed, he pressed on the button and another unit was added to the row of figures behind a little peephole, as on an odometer in a car. He sat down along the wall on the straw-covered floor so as not to bother the other two in their work.

The two oldest Negroes had been put inside; this was where the work was least tiring. They were both thin and wrinkled, with their pants rolled up over their calves, barefoot, their shirts disclosing the muscles of their arms, which floated a bit, like water, and their cheeks were covered with long white hairs. They vied with each other to catch the melons, take them over into the far end of the truck, and pile them delicately one on top of the other to get in the greatest number in the smallest space. "As if it were their own that they were loading," Mauro said to himself. From time to time they stole a glance at him. Mauro wasn't paying attention to what they were doing, but they became doubly attentive and alert because Mauro's attitude seemed suspect to them: they feared some trick on his part.

Mauro stayed there dozing for about an hour, his counter in his hand, and the truck was almost loaded when a rickety pickup truck arrived and stopped just behind the watermelon truck. A white man's big head, with a paralyzed grin on the face, just cleared the windshield. All the workers put aside their work with a single motion and crowded noisily around the door.

"Have a little patience, boys!" said a high, grating voice. The door opened and a tiny little hunchbacked man got out. He had a limp in his left leg. In the midst of the towering Negroes he looked like a little boy. Mauro couldn't tell how old he was, except that he was somewhere between twenty and fifty. He was wearing a khaki shirt and fancy perforated shoes that made him look even stranger among the men with bare feet.

"How many of 'em you got?" he asked Mauro with no surprise at his being there.

"836 or 37; I don't know if I counted the last one or not," he replied, looking at his counter.

The other man answered by whistling and went over to lean on the fender of the truck. He plunged his hand in the pocket of his pants and painfully took out a handful of coins. Mauro couldn't help noticing that his bowl-like hand with fingers bent back by gout were perfectly suited to the task. Without his having said anything, the Negroes lined up one behind the other for their pay.

"Hey, Vic, how much you giving me?" said the first one in line, one of the two oldest men who had worked inside the truck.

"Same as usual, you old fox. A dollar and thirty cents."

"How about the other truck? You forgetting that?"

"That'll come later; I'll have to do some figuring. It's not the same account because it's not for the same company."

"Don't forget now, and don't think I'll go off without it." The old man took the money, closed his hand around it, and went off grumbling, as if he felt like striking a blow with it.

Questions began to run down the line. Then Vic, the cripple, turned toward them and said in his high voice: "Don't worry, boys! You'll get all your pay before tonight, Vic guarantees it!"

The others said nothing. Vic seemed to be gloating, as if he were making fun of them, but Mauro realized that it was only because of his facial paralysis. In fact, he seemed distracted and tired, absolutely disinterested in what he was doing. It was as if he were trying to think of something else, pursue his dream apart, but it was plain that pain prevented him from doing so and brought him back to the task at hand. Each time that his stiff hand dug down into his pocket for the coins, he grimaced even more and his forehead wrinkled. Finally he took a notebook and a pencil out of his shirt pocket, wrote down some figures with his tongue sticking out, doubtless so that his clumsy fingers would not tremble too much as he wrote on the paper, then limped off toward the grocery store. The Negroes followed him. Handing out the pay served as a break in the work.

Mauro jumped down from the truck, caught up with Vic, and they entered the grocery store together, followed by Matt, who looked at the stranger without saying a word. The Negroes stopped at the door and sat down on the steps or the porch railing. The store was empty. It was more a dusty storehouse than a grocery store. There was no counter and no cash register. Cartons and boxes were piled up on the shelves and on the floor. His eyes never leaving Mauro, Matt got down several cans of beer and went out to take them to the Negroes talking outside in low voices. Mauro grabbed one of his arms as he passed by and took a roast beef and lettuce sandwich he left on the window sill. Vic had sat down on a packing case, pencil in hand, and was absorbed in his figures. When he had finished, Mauro asked him where everyone could have gone. "They're probably in the repair shed," Vic answered. "You can go in, it's that way," and he showed him the door in the back.

Mauro went out, and at one corner of the grocery he discovered a wooden shack with a tin roof. The door was open and he entered. A late-model black Studebaker, covered with a fine gray film, took up almost all the room in the place. The hood was open, and Dan, Steve, and the foreman whom he had replaced were working on the motor.

"Hi," George said as soon as he saw him come in. "You got something to eat, I hope?"

"Yes, I helped myself."

"It's taken longer than we thought. Excuse us. It wasn't ready."

"Are we leaving soon?"

"Right away. It's almost ready."

A bald giant in overalls, his belly sticking out, his torso nude and great pink beefsteaks on his arms, came into the shed.

"It must be time for you to leave," he said to George. In his blue overalls with straps and a bib, he could have been taken for a gardener in a comedy. Mauro guessed that it was little Matt's father.

"Mauro, this is Richard," George said, looking triumphant. "Richard, our hitchhiker."

Richard looked Mauro up and down with a kindly look and smiled. The others raised their heads from under the hood and looked at Mauro with a smile.

"Good for you, boys!" Richard said, giving him a big fatherly pat on the back. "Only George could have thought of a thing like that."

"George or Dan," the latter said ironically.

"Shut up," George replied. "Get busy and get this car ready to go instead of talking."

In the silence that followed, Mauro began to blush.

"In any case, as long as he's with you, you won't have any trouble getting to Georgia, I'll guarantee you."

"Come on," Mauro protested. "Steve or Dan certainly know more about fixing cars than I do, isn't that right, Dan?"

That made everybody laugh. Mauro was embarrassed and changed the subject: "Are you the one I pay for the beer and the sandwich?" he said to Richard.

"Put it on my bill," George interrupted. "We'll settle it on our way back."

"Whatever you like," Richard said.

"I'll pay next time," Mauro said to thank him.

"Whenever you like, son," George said.

"So you want to find work in Florida for the summer?" Richard said after a silence.

"I hope so."

"Find a job around here then," Richard said genially. "You wouldn't go wrong. We need people, this month especially."

"Maybe you're right," Mauro said. "I'll think it over."

"My boy, you're made to stay with us in the South, I can see it," Richard said with a laugh, pointing his index finger at him.

"We can get rolling," Dan said then, closing the hood. "You can go get the Chrysler, George."

Dan backed the car out; it sounded fine when he revved it up. Then George came back with the Chrysler. Mauro took his bag and put it in the other car, and Richard locked the double door of the shed.

"Have a good trip, kids," Richard said. "I'll have Vic get in touch with you when it's all right to come back. I know my sheriff."

"Let's hope so." George said, getting behind the wheel. "In any case, if he comes to visit you, we haven't seen each other since the kid got married."

"Too bad!" Richard sighed. "That's quite a while, don't you think?"

Mauro hesitated to laugh with everybody else, and smiled politely.

He had noticed as he got in the car that it was registered in Georgia. That had surprised him because they were still in South Carolina, still quite far from the Savannah River, which is the border between the two states. In fact, when he thought it over a little he decided that there was nothing strange about it, seeing that the closest big city must be Savannah, Georgia.

They drove out behind the grocery store past the little shaded yard and got back on the road. The black women were still there in a circle stringing beans, and when they saw the car, they suddenly began to whisper to each other. Another truck had arrived in the wide yard in front and the black men, who now had their white foreman back, had started loading melons again. Mauro waved good-by through the window, but none of them waved back. "They probably didn't see me," Mauro said to himself, disappointed.

Evening overtook them along the river. They had been following the Savannah River for an hour looking for a bridge. So far they had used only deserted, almost abandoned little country roads, and with all their detours they had taken a long time to cover a very small distance as the crow flies. George began to get nervous. But it was still light enough to see when once past Brinkley they crossed the iron bridge that spans the river in two sections. There was nothing to mark the border but a rusty road sign leaning on the superstructure of the bridge.

"We're there at last," George said once they had reached the other side. "We'll be in Savannah tonight."

"That's better," Steve said.

Dan didn't say anything. He wedged his knees up against the dashboard, turned around in his seat, and closed his eyes.

Just after the bridge they joined the main highway that they had had to leave to get to Richard's place. The road had become a real four-lane highway that ran straight on now, a treeless stretch between two oblique dirt banks covered with grass and weeds. Night fell, pink and soft, and came inside the car through the lowered windows. To Mauro, who was breathing in the cooler breeze as deeply as he could, the hot day was going away like a bad dream: the long, lonely wait on the outskirts of Jacksonboro, the anxiety in the car at first because nobody said anything, then the smell of the straw in the truck, the hostile eyes of the Negroes all disappeared behind him, in the wake the car left behind as it forged ahead at seventy miles an hour. There was nothing now but silence, the softness of the wind in his hair, in his shirt, and the pleasure of being with friends, together against the night. The rest was all gone. Everything except one last trace of the day, a dryness in the very back of his throat.

"I'm thirsty," Steve said.

"There's nothing left to drink," Dan warned, opening one eye. He had thrown the now-useless paper cups out with the empty bottles.

"We'll wet our whistles in Savannah, boys," George said. "Wait a while. You can bet your boots we'll drink in Savannah!" he added with a laugh.

"Meanwhile I still owe you for the beer and the

sandwich at Richard's," Mauro said then. "We can have
a drink on the way. That won't keep us from drinking
some more in Savannah."

"Sure," Steve said. "It's not our only chance."

"Not at all," Dan said. "I'm for a good rye."

"O.k.," George finally said. "We're not in a hurry any
more. I'll stop wherever you want, boys." And turning
to Mauro he added calmly: "It always comes out even
when you're pals, right?"

"Hey," Mauro said, "there's a place open over there."
He had caught sight of a neon-lighted façade above the
highway in the distance, on the right.

"We can always have a look at it."

"Yes, maybe we can go in."

George braked and parked the car on the side of
the road next to the slope that was fifteen yards or so
higher than the road, and led to a path that no doubt
went to the café. They climbed up through the grass.
In fact, it was a real street, the last little street of a
town, bordered by one-story wooden bungalows with
closed shutters, empty and shabby, as if an epidemic
had put the street in quarantine.

Only the café was lighted up. There were cars
parked in front of it, gleaming in the red neon of the
sign above the door; light filtered through the lowered
window blinds. Mauro crossed the road first and headed
toward the glass door. The three others slowed down
as they drew nearer, looking at each other question-
ingly. Suddenly George stopped and cried: "Don't go
in, Mauro; you're not supposed to!" But Mauro had
already pushed the door open and George's voice was
drowned out in the noise.

The room was half dark. Mauro hesitated a moment,

then went on toward the horseshoe-shaped counter with red leather stools fastened to the floor. The noise suddenly stopped altogether. In its place there was something strange in the air, something heavy and tense, as paralyzing as a threat. In the silence the ceiling fan, with unusually long blades, made a surprising amount of noise. A stool creaked as it pivoted on its chromed metal foot.

Mauro was still out of breath; he had run up the rather steep slope and his head was turning round and round. But he suddenly felt nailed to the spot by all the abnormally white pairs of eyes staring at him. He passed in review before the row of customers sitting along the counter, trying to find in these faces an explanation for his discomfort, feeling it at the tips of his fingers, at the tip of his tongue. His eyes then lighted on a little girl almost hidden by an ice-cream soda in front of her, who was looking at him open-mouthed, her spoon in her clenched fist suspended in mid-air, halfway between her mouth and her glass. He noticed that she was black, perhaps because of her little pearl earrings and the purple ribbon in her frizzy hair, and he stood there looking at her with an empty look, as if he were trying to recall something in his mind. The young woman in a green dress sitting next to the little girl leaned over toward her, and with that burning and broken voice of black women that seems to come up from their belly, said in the silence: "Come on, eat. What you lookin' at that white man for?"

Mauro gave a start. He looked around him and his shirt stuck to his back. He was the only white in the place. He had gone into black territory; he had violated the border. He gave a little cough to put a good face on it, stammered something in apology, and slowly retreated toward the door, his eyes straight ahead. He did not dare turn his back. Fortunately he had left the door half open for the others behind him. When he was outside he slammed the door, caught his breath, took several breaths of the cool air, and still shocked and dumfounded at his mistake, he went back toward the others.

Mauro felt a terrible pain in his face, in his crushed nose. He instinctively raised his arms to protect himself; a body blow to the stomach wrenched a cry from him, as brief and hoarse as a spasm. He fell to his knees, with the back of his neck lowered; he wasn't about to let himself fall yet. He recognized George's black shoes.

"So you wanted to turn us in?" George murmured, bending over him.

"What did you tell them? We don't want any trouble out of you."

Behind him in the middle of the street, Dan's eyes bored through the dark. Outside of the half-moon of purple light in front of the café, the street was dark and deserted. At the edge of the slope Steve was rejoicing, feverishly repeating in a half-whisper: "What difference does it make, Mr. Spott? We're past the border. We can let him go now." He didn't dare either to shout or to approach Mauro. Steve wasn't a loud-mouth. He just didn't want his presence to be forgotten.

George was barely listening. The blows had calmed him. He smiled as he watched Mauro squatting on his knees, his hands clutching his belly, a ball of air blocked in his throat. He murmured something with his mouth, like a fish out of water. "Turn you in, turn you in . . . you're crazy . . ."

His eyes sought out Dan's to appeal to him. He at least would understand something that was only a misunderstanding, an error on his part, that they couldn't hold it against him because he'd happened to go in there.

"Dan! Dan! What did I do to you?" He hadn't yet caught his breath and was grinding his teeth on nothing. This was as hard for him as it would have been to shout.

Dan sniggered. "Maybe he wanted to give us away to the niggers, but he did us a favor all the same. We can always thank him for the favor, right, George?"

"Why not, Dan? If he hasn't caught on yet, it's because he's a gourd-head. He should go back where he came from."

Mauro shook his head desperately. He felt a warm breath of whisky pass over his face. Dan had grabbed him by the shirt. He tried to push him away with his hands, leaning on him with all his strength.

"Come on, be good," Dan said without anger, pushing him away. "That's right, we do have to thank you for the little trip we took together."

"Dan, you're out of your mind. What's gotten into you?" Mauro stammered.

"Wait a minute. I'm not crazy at all. We had to take a trip, you see, but not by ourselves. Something happened up there."

Dan spoke very softly as if he were telling a little boy a story to keep him quiet.

"There was a nigger that was agitating on the farms around us. He talked about organizing all the niggers in the neighborhood, self-defense they call it, and doing what Mr. Williams* did in Monroe. And then they discovered a rifle in his house. Then we had to go by the nigger's place and arrange for him never to use a rifle again, you see what I mean? Rifles are dangerous. They scare me. Then we had to take a little trip somewhere and wait for things to simmer down."

"I don't see what you mean about a favor," Mauro said. He had gotten up and was facing Dan now.

Dan burst out laughing. "No doubt about it, fellas, this guy should go back where he came from," he said finally, turning his head toward the others.

He turned back around to Mauro:

"Because the niggers gave the police up there our description, can you imagine? They said they'd seen three whites drive away in a red Chevvy. Isn't that something? But the police don't have anything on four whites in a black Studebaker. It's no business of theirs."

Mauro felt a great emptiness in his head. He couldn't seem to get what Dan was saying through his head.

"Hey, come on, Dan," George yelled from a distance. "We've lost enough time with that sucker. He's got friends here to take care of him."

"So we'll leave the nigger-lover with the niggers,"

* The reference is to Robert Williams, the organizer of Negro self-defense militias in Monroe, South Carolina. Accused by the FBI and pursued by the Ku Klux Klan, he fled to Cuba in August, 1961.

Dan said. "Go get his bag out of the car, Steve." And he added for Mauro's benefit: "You can tell 'em whatever you want now. I'd like to see the white that would listen to you without popping you one in the kisser. Don't forget, the cops here are white."

And he joined George again on the other side of the road at the edge of the slope.

When Mauro saw that they were going to leave him there by himself, with his face bleeding, in the deserted street, in this country with strange rules, he pulled himself together, gave a start, and yelled at their backs at the top of his lungs:

"Wait for me! Don't leave me! Dan! I'm not yellow!"

George spit on the ground and kept on walking. But Dan turned around suddenly, with his fists clenched. He came back over to Mauro, who hadn't budged. He was still busy wiping his blood-covered mouth and face with his hand, and misjudged how fast the punch was coming. This time Mauro gave a long bellow and lost his balance. He got another punch on the mouth, then right afterward two quick cuts of Dan's elbow on his collarbone and his stomach, and he fell backward against the glass of the café.

"I hope he's had enough this time," Dan said as he took off.

As he fell, Mauro had had the time to see, for the fraction of a second, the row of Negroes lined up behind the glass, watching him from the café, silent, indifferent, motionless. They had raised the blinds to see. Then the neon sign went out and all the Negroes filed out of the place. Someone inside put iron gratings over the windows. The little girl with the purple ribbon passed by Mauro weeping, hurriedly dragged along by an elegant Negro couple with brilliantined hair. No crowd formed, there were no shouts, no horns honking, just a quick tacit understanding. Mauro heard the rubber-dampened noise of doors slamming, and the cars took off one after the other with a soft purr.

A man with shining eyes, who had left the place after everyone else and looked younger than the others, left the last little group of Negroes and came toward him with his shirt-tail sticking out.

"Can I do anything for you?" he said.

Mauro tried to get up on one elbow to see who was talking to him, but it was no use. He felt glued to the earth, with a nauseating taste of salt in his mouth. There was too much for him to do now to bother about not crying there in front of them. He shook his head.

"There's nothing in it for you," said one of the two men who had stayed behind. "Come on then, hurry up."

"You may be right at that, boys," said the man who had gone over to Mauro, looking at him. And he joined the others.

"This guy's their business, right?" the third man said. "If they don't put the blame on us, we'll be lucky."

All three disappeared down the slope in the direction of the highway. A few minutes had sufficed to empty the place completely. The whole street had returned to shadow, like a dead person.

Mauro was alone now, stretched out motionless on his back, his face to the first stars. In the west, violet slits still barred the sky. The night was slowly binding up its wounds. Soon you wouldn't be able to see a thing. Down below on the highway, the trucks, big insects with severed legs, climbed with an exhausted hum and their headlights probed the night like antennas. Each time one passed, a pencil of white light passed over the surface of the slope and lighted up Mauro's hand, raised in an intermittent gesture begging for help.

And then, like a desire to burst into tears, the desire for something else besides punches, mistrust, loneliness and the shame of being alone, and all the strange rules of this life mounted in his throat. A gray and white city, where there is no sea, passed before his eyes in the night—could this ever be understood by the others down there who were waiting for him with their pockets full of bills, those who were sleeping on the ground waiting for him behind the station, where on sunny days the buzzing of flies on garbage drowns out the voices of the naked kids, those who pulled at each night to get the waiting over with, could they understand that it was not so easy to live if you couldn't speak to anybody you wanted to, and if you couldn't push a door without first looking to see whether it said WHITE ONLY or COLORED ONLY?

But Mauro did not cry. He too had just passed a border, and had the confused feeling that he would not come back across it. He had never before experienced such a complicity with some unknown something or someone, perhaps with the stars above him, perhaps also with the men with bright eyes whose presence he was aware of around him in the dark along this road, in the cities along this road, and in the shanties far from any road. He wanted to smile at someone, but there was no one with him. Then with his eyes open wide, he simply smiled at the sky as if it were an old pal from back home after you've lost track of all the others. At this Georgia sky the color of a bleeding night.

A Young Man
in the Know

She was just coming in when I called her. Yes, the operation went fine, they'd put her to sleep, it was an apartment that had special equipment, she was unconscious only a short time. They were very nice to her afterward, they'd been great, she had· given them the money and they'd brought her back home in a car, a white Alfa-Romeo Giulietta, can you imagine? All that said very fast, in a toneless voice, going on and on, as if to avoid questions, to get rid of this bothersome past that was too close as quickly as possible. And she went on immediately:

"I'd like to see you, you know. It's not much fun being all alone in this huge apartment. My aunt has dreadful taste. . . . Is there anything else you have to do tonight?"

"Of course not, since I came home just on account of you. You really don't think . . ."

"Well, I'll leave the key under the doormat for you. I'm going to bed; they told me I ought to. I really don't feel like getting up again."

"Right. And don't move around. . . . Sleep if you feel like it, I won't wake you up."

"No, no, I'll wait for you. . . . You know the address, don't you?"

"Yes. See you in a little while."

Whew! I was about to suffocate in that stuffy telephone booth, with its smell of brilliantine and oily hair that gets you by the throat in summer in public phone booths. It wasn't much better outside, but I was really quite happy. The business with Sylvie was over. I didn't have three thousand francs in my pocket, but Monday I'd get the forty thousand I'd earned with my surveys in the suburbs; just three days to go. Enough to get by for a while, find a new room (the landlady where I was staying had asked me for the key back a week ago because I was two months behind and brought in people "who weren't very decent sorts," as she put it). This time of year, it's still easy to find a place; everybody's cleared out. I could even give Sylvie a little money. She'd paid for the whole operation, without asking me for a thing—but how, in fact, did she get the money? She doesn't have a job. Her family is well off, but obviously she didn't say a word to them. As a matter of fact, she hadn't said anything to me, neither that she didn't dare go through with it nor that she was ashamed to ask me for the money. I already owed her a lot.

It was Saturday at six o'clock now. The heat poured out from everywhere, from the sidewalk, from the walls, from the people. I had just enough money to take a taxi and buy a bottle of wine in a grocer's to surprise her, give her a present. What I really wanted was to make the night a special one for Sylvie and me, our last night together: I didn't have the least desire to see her again and wanted to leave her with a nice memory. Not that she'd clung to me, far from it, but I'd had enough, that's all.

The streets filed by behind the taxi windows, hot and deserted. Summer was really here. Paris looked like a big, hollow, grayish fossil, with its succession of empty streets, its silent façades with all the shutters closed. A greater number than there were births, I'd read in a medical magazine. And the ones that weren't success-ful, the complications, the infections, the destruction of organs, sterility. Funny though. She hadn't hung back too much, she was almost proud that it had hap-pened to her, or curious. At her age, it was the first time.

It was hard to breathe even inside a car, above all on account of the gray implacable dust that makes you all sticky and even clings to the inside of your nose. The boulevards were full of people from the provinces or Americans who were walking around doing nothing, burping beer, their shirts unbuttoned with a dark half-moon under their arms and a little straw hat shading their eyes. Poor people, I feel sorry for them. I would have liked to go to the country like everyone else. But I couldn't drop Sylvie right after the operation, you know. . . . The country's very nice, moreover. But you have to get somebody to invite you, and that's not so easy. I'm just joking though!

The sixteenth arrondissement; it looked like a pile of dead stones. A real desert, everyone gone . . . to the Normandy coast or somewhere else. I was the only one left, with my bottle of champagne in my arms, looking tacky. Nonetheless I gave a two-hundred-franc tip to the driver, a fat little man, his shirt wet in the back, his face all red, who just breathed in through his mouth with a slight noise, like a fish.

She was just going to sleep. When she saw me come into the room, she sat up in bed; I went over to kiss her and she played hostess of the place from the depths of her bed, with embarrassed smiles. I glanced into the other rooms. There was nothing to be embarrassed about, because it was rather an amusing sort of apartment. It was on the sixth floor but it looked like a basement apartment. You would have thought you were in a museum in the provinces. It was cool, spacious, and very dark. Nothing had probably been changed in the place since maybe 1890. The armchairs, for example, were not anything to sit in; there were slipcovers on most of them, and they seemed to be screwed to the rugs. And light like in an aquarium playing over everything: there wasn't much sunlight, what with the shutters, the glass, the yellowed tulle curtains, the dark purple or brown or dark green cretonne drapes—not the gayest sort of thing in the world. On the walls was an eruption of old lacquered paintings that were all black, so that all you could see of them was their enormous frames of gilded wood. The gildings were as rococo as could be. In fact—there, I've got it now: it was a museum of trinkets. There were knickknacks everywhere, on the consoles, on the mantels, on the tops of the radiators, on the tables: mythological bronzes, Lady Lucks balancing on little wheels, lady huntresses, lady avengers, ladies setting the world on fire, all naked, cupids in every possible position and material, in terra cotta, in iron, in gilded wood, in bronze, and clocks that weren't running, plates, jars, not to mention the porcelains—you know, the sort of pink and green things with depraved-looking shepherdesses who hold out little flowers in gilded metal, brass, or copper. The whole place, moreover, smelled like an old cupboard.

It was nice in her room. She had picked out a very bare bedroom, doubtless one that was no longer being used, at the very end of the hall, with a big square bed. The shutters were closed, and a dim bed lamp was lighted.

"It's lucky too that I can have peace here," she said to me. "My aunt's on vacation and left me her apartment."

"Did you tell her why?" I was afraid the family would get mixed up in it.

"No. I told them it was so I could work in peace."

"How about your parents?"

"They've left too, and shut up the house. It's rather handy for them to have me here . . . but let's not talk about that any more, if you'd rather not. . . . It's nice you're here. I'm very happy, you know. . . ."

It was no use protesting that that was the way things

should be and even a pleasure for me; she insisted absolutely that she was happy. I couldn't do a thing about it. I hadn't told her that I'd been thrown out on the street. In general, I told her as little as possible about what I was doing. Luckily, she was timid.

Her long hair fell smoothly across the pillow. She must have combed it before I arrived. There in her bed her little girl's face just peeked over the stiff white sheets; her slanting green eyes like a ferdelance's, her thick lips, her prominent cheekbones made me think more than ever of, you know . . . those Mexican or maybe Indian statues that are very flat and have precious stones instead of eyes. She smiled at me fearfully beneath the lamp. It was as if she feared I would give her a talking-to.

"Does it hurt?"

"No, no, not too much. . . . Just a little tired, that's all."

"Well, it's over now!" I said with a smile to clear the air. "That's always the way it is. Here, I've brought this bottle to drink together."

"You know, I really don't want any. . . ."

I insisted that she take some, because it would make her feel better, make her high, and she finally agreed to have some. As I was looking for the glasses in the hall, I wondered what was the matter with her. There was something that wasn't right, that wasn't the way it usually was. She had a happy and very sad look that I couldn't describe to you . . . an absent smile . . . as if she were trying to hide some sort of disappointment. . . . I had never seen her like that in all the time I'd known her. Three or four months, I don't remember exactly. It was strange.

Happily, the cork was a diversion. The foam ran all over the rug. I sat down on the bed, and we clinked glasses. She drank a mouthful leaning on the edge of the bed with her eyes closed, grimaced, then smiled at me again. The second mouthful she spit back into her glass, blushing. Then I told her to stop, not to force herself, that it was just to please her, but that it wasn't important. She lay back down, apologizing. I had the whole bottle to myself. The champagne was warm, but you know me, when it's that hot I get nervous thirsts, terrible thirsts. I can't control myself. I spilled plenty of it on the sheets, on my shirt, but I almost finished the bottle. She kept giving me a distant smile, without saying anything.

I asked her how long she was supposed to stay in bed. She should stay in bed for about a week, according to what they'd said. She perked up a little talking about the future. To hear her talk that way, you'd think she was playing a trick on her family and everybody. "My parents won't know a thing about it. What they don't know won't hurt them! and then bang, we'll begin all over again!" she finally said, bursting out laughing. It made me feel great to see her so happy; suddenly I began laughing too. I'd had the champagne of course. But it was a wholehearted laugh.

Suddenly I remembered. It was like a cold shower. I shut up all of a sudden and looked at the rug. Then she looked at me, completely disconcerted.

"No, you see, darling," I said to her (it was hard to say darling, but it was now or never), "we have to be a little more careful. We musn't do things like we did before. . . . You're great, you know. But I'm not sure if I'm"—I was going to say "the kind of guy you need," but just then I felt her looking at me so hard, so fearfully I really felt it, on my skin, and I saw her face that had suddenly grown serious, white, again, with all the pain in her belly suddenly mounting to her eyes. . . . It's silly, but I lowered my voice a tone and finished my sentence in a murmur. I didn't want her to cry. She took my hand; hers was burning. I was suddenly afraid that she had guessed. . . . Then I took her in my arms and kissed her gently on the lips; I could see her damp eyes very close. I dropped my head down onto the hollow in her neck as far as it would go. I wanted her to forget. I didn't want her to cry, you understand. That would have ruined everything. I would have hated myself too much for having made her cry at a time like that.

It's not my way to drop girls when they've just had an abortion. I think that's disgusting.

She turned her face toward the wall and buried it in the pillow. She was holding me in her arms, very tightly. She didn't want me to see her cry, or else it was simply that she was tired. But I couldn't help feeling just a little bit ashamed, ashamed on account of her, on account of me too, if you like, ashamed on account of everything, at the thought that her whole life was going to be like that, without protesting, without answering, without even asking the questions that came to her lips. I could have insulted her, and it wasn't that I didn't feel like it, I assure you, I could have yelled at her right to her face that she was beginning to be a drag on me, that I was sick of it, of her and her nice little loving—and she would have turned toward the wall and begged my pardon. Not out of . . . love, if you insist on pronouncing that word. No. Maybe only out of politeness. I had never seen a single gesture of anger, or of hate from this girl, never seen her keep her distance, never heard an ugly word out of her: nothing. Sweetness itself. For seventeen years she had been taught to act decently. Sometimes you feel like stepping all over people like that, right?

Then I began to talk to her about what it was like outside, altogether too nice, told her that she had really hit on the right moment, that we couldn't take a little walk down in the street now. I had to change the subject. She must have answered that she would really prefer being out with me, or something like that. . . . We could have gone to the movies, in an air-conditioned theater on the Champs-Élysées. Or gone to spend the weekend in the country. "What would we use for money?" I felt like answering her.

"Well, anyway, you're here . . . what am I complaining about?" she asked me, taking my head in her two hands. There was no reason to get upset, now was there? She perhaps went on in that tone of voice for a long time, but either I had drunk too much or she was talking too softly, or both, but all I heard was a mumble. To tell the truth, I think I didn't really have much of an idea of what I was doing there. I got up and said that everything was just fine, that I was very happy and she was too, and that I'd stay over and sleep there, or something like that. I remember that she got a little upset, and made some suggestions, though I didn't understand very well what they were all about. . . . She quietly dropped off to sleep. I too felt as heavy as a big weight. The bed in the next room was made up.

I left the door between the two rooms half open and flopped down on the sheets with all my clothes on. I hadn't even had dinner.

It took me a long time to realize. I sleep too soundly. A discreet little panting noise . . . something that wavered between a sob and a muffled little laugh. People are right to talk about laughing till you cry. I thought I was dreaming, you see. The voice came from a long way off, all out of breath. "Gilbert . . . Gilbert . . ." When I heard my name I really woke up. Once on my feet, it didn't take me long to see what was up. She was half naked, lying on her back with her head thrown stiffly back. She was twisting the sheets that had come untucked with her fist, with her nightgown pulled up as far as her belly. She apparently wore a nylon nightgown even in summer, for decency's sake. And between the V of her half-open thighs there was a big stain on the sheet. The pillow was on the floor, and the bolster too. She saying "Gilbert . . . Gilbert . . ." over and over between her teeth, in the middle of hiccoughs, of little dry rattles, of silences while she caught her breath again. My God, I wish I could forget that voice! When she saw me, she hid her pubis with her two hands. Maybe to stop herself, block up the hole, prevent herself from hemorrhaging. A strange idea anyway. Very soon the blood began to seep out between her fingers.

"How long has this been? . . . Why didn't you wake me up?"

"For a long time . . . I called you softly, I shouted . . . you didn't answer. I didn't want to wake you up."

I pulled up the sheets and wiped her face with them. She had beads of sweat on her forehead that made her hair stick together in ringlets. Funny her fever went up so high, when I look back on it. And all of a sudden, with no warning. I also wiped her red sticky hands with the top sheet. And I stayed there in the dark bedroom for a long moment, my arms dangling, not knowing what in hell to do. If you want a comparison, imagine the bottom of a well with water slowly climbing up the smooth walls and yourself down inside. In the bottom of my well it was two o'clock in the morning.

It finally occurred to me to call Claude, a pal of mine who's studying medicine. I should really have thought of him sooner, for I'd already had to call on him for help for other messes of this sort, and it had always turned out O.k. But with Sylvie I couldn't get in gear. My head was running in neutral. Luckily Claude answered the phone at the other end. He was in bed with a girl, but when I told him what it was all about in a few words, he told me he'd drive over right away. I could hardly talk, and could barely remember the address of the apartment house. I said to myself to calm myself down: "He'll be here in a few minutes. He'll give her injections, the hemorrhage will stop, and her fever will go down. Come on, old boy, tomorrow morning it'll all be over."

She called me from the other end of the hall, but I stayed where I was, sitting in the living room on a chair with a slipcover in front of the telephone, not able to budge. With my mouth dry. With an empty feeling in my stomach. I finally tumbled to the fact that what was wrong with me was called a hangover. This discovery somewhat restored my self-confidence. I must still be drunk, but not enough, alas, to not give a damn about the whole thing. The chandelier with its little oval bulbs was turning round and round above my head. The ceiling kept receding, or rather rolling upward, and it made me dizzy. She stopped shouting when she saw me come back into the room. I stayed at the door to make sure I wouldn't fall. Suffering, helplessness, humiliation, and I don't know what, all made her face tense and kept her from shouting or sobbing. Something had to be done while waiting for Claude, finding medicine, for example. I didn't find anything in the bathroom. I began running all through the damned apartment. I discovered even more rooms, with plush divans, purple sofas, chandeliers on the floor even, not to mention all the other things. When I couldn't find the light switches, I bumped into chairs and walls and knick-knacks in the dark, and had a great time. Things fell from all over with a bang, like firecrackers. I systematically opened all the cupboards, stuffed to bursting, unimaginable. They must not have been aired very often, because all I had to do was open one of them halfway and it immediately poured its cargo of entrails smelling of naphtha out into my arms: yellowed linens, old tablecloths, miscellaneous kitchen equipment, lamp bases, old books, split pillows, lace with holes in it, odds and ends of dishes, pieces of rabbit fur, hats with veils, telephone books and who knows what else. All of it piled up with no rhyme or reason. And can't you just see me getting hit over the head with all that stuff, getting my face smashed with turbot-kettles and old shoes, feeling as stupid and decrepit as an elderly paralytic? And to think that it was her old oyster of an aunt who'd unloaded all that on my back just to make me flounder in it! I was so on edge I was just about ready to split the scene and forget the whole thing. You don't see the funny side of things while they're happening.

I went back to her bedside, empty-handed. All I could do was dust myself off and count the bumps and bruises I'd collected in the various cupboards. I don't know how she managed to combine the two, but she was groaning and losing blood and yet she managed to smile at me the whole while and calm me by the way she looked at me. I paced around the room, my mind only half clear. All I was waiting for was for her mother to arrive. She was going to appear suddenly in the middle of the night, surprise the two of us there together, with me at Sylvie's bedside watching her insides slowly emptying out with an annoyed look on my face. Mama would tear her hair, take heaven as witness and her daughter in her arms to get her away from the dirty assassin, profiteer, seducer, rake, the whole bit, rounding up all the solid citizens and decent families in the world to serve as witnesses. That would have been perfect. When you come right down to it, I must have a taste for cheap melodrama. Sylvie at least wasn't upset. She smiled her nice little smile to reassure me.

. . . Then Claude arrived. The sight of him standing in the doorway, tall and straight and thin, with his long impassible face, his fringe of black beard, his untroubled eyes, and his little bag in his hand, calmed me down. I had probably lost my head. Sylvie also seemed to be reassured when she saw him, even though she didn't know him. Claude examined her unhurriedly, questioned her on the conditions under which the operation had taken place, took her temperature. He yawned; all this bored him, I suppose. She had a temperature of over 103. He then told me to boil the syringe and the needle, and gave her an injection to combat the infection and make her fever go down. He gave her some pills for the hemorrhaging, which was still going on, though not quite so badly. When she had gone to sleep, Claude dragged me off into the next room.

"I've only got one dose, pal. And she ought to have the stuff every two hours until her fever goes down. . . ."

"But everything's closed. In three hours it'll be five and some. . . ."

"There has to be one pharmacy that stays open in the neighborhood. Go find it, you've got plenty of time," he said to me in a detached tone. "I'll use the time to study for once." And he pulled a thick bound book out of his bag, and another small one from his pocket that I hadn't seen.

"You see, I look ahead," he continued with a smile. ". . . When you come right down to it, it's good you got me out of bed. . . ."

"It's always a drag to leave somebody when you're in bed together, isn't it? Was she good?"

"Well, *I* like sleeping alone, you know," he said, falling into the armchair.

"Watch her room anyway. . . ."

"Sure, sure. . . ."

I got my jacket and was about to go.

"Oh, I forgot! They'll ask you for a prescription. Say

you didn't know that, that it's urgent; use your head.
I can't give you one. I didn't bring any hospital forms
with me. Go ahead, and good luck."

"Same to you!"

"I'll expect you within two hours, not a second more
than that!"

It was pleasantly warm outside. On these July nights
in Paris, it does my heart good just to feel the air on my
skin, the little warm breaths that pass over you, smelling
faintly of musk. . . . It's marvelous to be out late at a
time like that, isn't it? Marvelous, and sad at the same
time. You feel that you're very close to people on
account of the way things smell, the warmth, and you
feel like holding somebody's hand, but basically nothing
has changed and you don't dare. When you're alone on
the street in summer, you feel much more alone than
in winter. . . . But never mind. The fact is that all that
got me in shape to walk again. I was happy not to be
asleep. At the pharmacy nearby, I noted down the address of the pharmacies that were still open. I went
the rounds of all of them; they were all closed. It was
just between the time the Saturday night ones closed
and the Sunday morning ones opened, I suppose. I
should have taken Claude's car, but it was too far to
go back. Once I thought I saw a green cross lighted
up; I ran, ran as fast as I knew how along the—wait
a minute, yes, the rue de la Pompe—and when I got
there the light had gone out and they'd just closed.
I came back by the Trocadéro and the avenue Kléber,
catching my breath as I went along. There were no taxis,
and nobody around. Just dogshit on the ground and the
smell of the chestnut trees. But there were still people

on the Champs-Élysées. It felt great being there. There were sports cars there, and the place was full of girls, especially at this time of night, with low-cut dresses and bouffant skirts they could hike up easily. The wakes of their perfume cross behind them and it drives you mad. Take it from me, at that hour you can't make out. Except for the hookers, all of them are shacking up with somebody. I went straight to the drugstore, where there was a line in the little glassed-in pharmacy, you know the one. A little guy in a white smock tried to make trouble for me. I said I'd forgotten to bring the prescription with me, that it was too late to go home and get it because they were going to close. I must have given him a hard time, because he shrugged his shoulders and finally gave me the damned penicillin. I got a little wind back, shook one or two hands in the restaurant, and left. There were some guys there who were already tanned, can you imagine?—as if they'd just come back from their vacations, and I hadn't even left yet! I told myself that it was time to get some money, for sure this time, if I wanted to buy a decent car and a couple of passable Italian suits. To think that I'd been forced to sell all my stuff like that to pay back a broad who threatened to take me to court, can you imagine!

I was dying of thirst. Since I still had some of the dough that Sylvie had given me for the medicine left, I went to have a drink at the snackbar at the Lido. Everybody was laughing loudly and doing some hard drinking. The neon, the noise, the music—it must have been Miles Davis on the jukebox—did my heart good. I was amused at the thought of that prehistoric apartment I'd left; I really didn't want to go back, you see, to Sylvie, who was pissing blood on top of everything else; it wasn't very funny. I had a hard time making myself leave the place, but it was getting late. And who do you think I met as I went by the Comédie Française? Patrick and Jean-Marc, no, you probably don't know them, they're pals of mine. I was about to go by them without seeing them, it would have been better, but they wave and wave at me, and Patrick comes over to me with a big grin on his face.

"You couldn't have come at a better time, pal," he says to me. "Are you alone?"

They'd just dragged three girls out of a frightful place where they play tangoes; stenographers, not too bad. It was too nice a night for the girls to go home to bed. Except that there were only two of them and the third one wanted to stick around. I was their savior. Friendship is a matter of life and death to stenos. They were willing to go to bed, but it was the three of them together or nothing. They explained all this to me very pompously, which meant that they'd had quite a bit to drink. I went along with them then. All six of us got in the car, a big Rover with a mahogany instrument panel, to go to Jean-Marc's place. They'd gotten past the stage of the social graces. They were laughing over nothing and embracing each other to their hearts' content. But I couldn't seem to get with it. The third girl, a not very pretty brunette with lots of candy-pink lipstick on, had taken my arm and was waiting for me to join the party. I had my nose to the window; I don't know what I was thinking of. Suddenly I went to get my cigarettes in my pocket, and felt the box of pills in my hand. It all came back to me then, I turned as red as a beet, asked

65

Patrick to stop, mumbling an excuse, and jumped out onto the pavement, barely missing being hit by a big Rolls that indignantly swerved and braked right afterward. We were still on the Champs-Élysées, near the Étoile. I ran then and could hear them calling after me, but I didn't turn around, I ran and ran till I was out of breath. I saw passers-by looking at me, and a few of them even stopped. Dawn was breaking; it was after five. I felt like vomiting, and my legs felt as if they were made of cotton wool. Then I got scared.

Everything was ringing in my head like horns honking: the neon, the noise, the windows, the headlights. And floating above all this commotion, Sylvie's damp eyes staring at me.

Claude was waiting for me in the foyer. He looked nervous and his features were drawn. He took the box of pills from my hand without saying a word. He must not have shut his eyes for one second. In the bedroom Sylvie was half awake and stammering incomprehensible things: that she had to get up, take advantage of the nice weather, not be late. "Late where?" I asked her, but she wouldn't answer. She kept on muttering: "Gilbert, Gilbert, let's hurry . . . get ready, Gilbert."

He gave her a second injection and a *gardénal* and she went back to sleep. She had almost stopped hemorrhaging. The spots on the towel that was under her in the bed weren't getting any bigger. Claude asked me if I knew how to give injections. No, naturally I didn't. I thought I had already told him that. Then he explained to me, in an embarrassed way, that he would have liked to go home; his exam was coming up soon, and he hadn't slept for two nights now. "You might as well stay here," I told him, "there are plenty of beds." He could wait till the next day at any rate. He replied that it already was the next day, and settled down with his books in one of the innumerable bedrooms opening onto the hall, because according to him he was too tired to sleep. He grumbled and swore and stormed at what I was making him do. He sent the bedspread, the cushions, and the comforter flying to the other end of the room and finally lay down. Sylvie was sleeping on her back with her mouth half open, her face relaxed, and her hands stretched out flat on the sheets. She was sleeping soundly. She made you think of a little girl playing dead in a pantomime of a wake such as children dream up. So I went to bed too. Sooner or later I had to get some sleep somehow.

What suddenly woke me with a start was the sound of a chair falling, a heavy, dull thud. I came to suddenly this time, all at once. It seemed as if I had barely slept at all. On the night table was a note from Claude, saying he had gone out to get some coffee and not to worry. You could say that again! Sylvie's bed was empty. I heard groans in the hall. It was her, crawling on her knees in the dark, with her hands on the walls and blood on her face. The way I understand it, she had gotten up to go to the bathroom and once there she had gotten dizzy and fallen head first onto the tile floor. The shock made her suddenly come to again. She got up, but when she saw herself in the mirror with her forehead open she really fainted. She didn't know how long it was before she came to. The cut was quite deep, and her skin had split across half her forehead. She told me she didn't feel much, that if she had fainted—I remember her words very well —it was because she hadn't recognized herself in the mirror and thought she was disfigured, and not because of the pain. To reassure her I told her that it didn't matter as long as we had stitches taken in it right away. We had been talking without budging from the hall, the two of us kneeling on the floor in the dark, with me holding her so she wouldn't fall. I pulled her to her feet and almost had to carry her, with one arm around her waist and the other leaning against the wall. She was very heavy, especially since we couldn't walk two abreast, the hallway was too narrow and the waxed floor made us slip; she finally got hold of the doorknob and I put her down on the bed. I had gotten blood all over me, on the front of my shirt and down my pants. She had too, and her nightgown was all splattered with blood. Bits of hair had gotten stuck in the cut and coagulated. She curled up in the bed and turned toward the wall, with her head in her arms. She didn't want me to see the gash in her forehead; she turned sullen and whined softly. She was afraid that I would see her disfigured, ugly, sick. . . . When she finally turned toward me she was bright red with shame and didn't dare look me in the eye.

It was a real mess. There was blood everywhere. It seemed to me as if the least thing she did would turn against her, that everything that we could try to do would only bring on catastrophe all the sooner. She had begun to hemorrhage again down below too; and blood was gushing out. As it dried it got black and the sheets and the pillow crackled. I couldn't understand the whole thing. Blood is strange. It makes you afraid and leaves you stunned with surprise, both at the same time, because it's anonymous, impersonal. It can come out of anything. It finally doesn't even have a color. It was beyond me, but I wondered what use there was in trying madly, in struggling, in plugging her up. Maybe I get discouraged too easily, but I had no more desire to stir from where I was than if I were watching a landslide or an earthquake from a distance. I would serve as a witness; you always need one in cases like that. I would be the one who would notify the authorities afterward, who would give journalists the first report, the guy that you see next day on the first page of the papers, full-face or in a three-quarter profile, with a dazed look, blinded by the flashbulbs and perhaps by the stroke of luck he's had as well. That's what I told myself. Period. . . . I must be something of a fatalist at heart.

She for her part said to me, looking somewhere else, in a grumpy tone of voice: "Don't bother about me. It'll all take care of itself. You're tired."

"I'm not going to leave you in this state, am I now? You haven't seen what you look like.".

And she said: "I've already taken your Saturday. You must have something else to do. Leave if you want to. I can take care of things all right all by myself. Claude's going to be back."

Good lord, she had become downright affectionate! She was taking me for her father or her big brother. If only she'd hated me, called me names, pommeled me with her fists, told me I was a bastard—that would have relieved me a lot. Instead of her modest little look, her look of a little girl caught doing something bad, who doesn't want to make trouble and who was beginning to get on my nerves, that's what. . . .

Impossible to leave her alone five minutes to go hunt for Claude in the neighborhood cafés. He wouldn't be gone long anyway. It was no use my changing the compresses, the blood kept seeping through. The tatters of flesh around the gash were turning black, like the pink flesh inside. It absolutely had to be stitched up or there would be the risk of infection, not to mention the infection in her belly that hadn't ended yet; she was still trembling from fever. It was no use for her to protest that it wasn't worth calling a doctor in, that it was Sunday, that he wouldn't come for such a small matter; she finally gave me the number of her family doctor. Deep down in her heart she wanted him to come, but she was balking just for appearance's sake. The trouble was that people don't get their heads gashed just like that; we'd have to make up some story. We agreed that we'd say that she'd had a dizzy spell when she got up because it was her regular period, that she'd then phoned me so as not to bother a doctor and that I was the one responsible for calling him in. . . . "Moreover," she added, "all we'll ask him to do is sew me up; he's not paid to ask questions"—this in a firm tone that surprised me, or maybe it was just the tone of a little girl who was accustomed to servants. It bothered me nonetheless. I was afraid it would seem funny to him that I was the one who called. I wasn't anxious to be seen with Sylvie, especially in circumstances like that. But there was no other solution. After all, this doctor was no business of mine. You'll tell me that Sylvie was no business of mine either. Well, don't you believe it; deep down I was ready to do anything to help her. I put on my voice for great occasions, superior, serious, and slow, when I talked to the doctor on the phone. I passed myself off as more or less a friend of her aunt. It went over perfectly, and he told me he'd be right over, in a very polite, solicitous voice. It occurred to me that we might be able to ask him to help us for the rest of it too. . . . The guy might be our salvation.

She had taken off the bolster and put her head down flat to stop the blood from flowing. Tears rolled gently down her face, but you couldn't say that she was crying. It was fever or fatigue. I was bushed myself. It would have relaxed me to cry, if only I'd been able to. She was very pale, with her arms lying at her sides. The sheets showed her exact outline. I took her hand, and in my same telephone voice told her to be patient, that tomorrow she'd think no more about it, that life would be even better after this rough moment, that you have to pay for everything, for love among other things. I didn't have to make it up, it all came out by itself. It was as if somebody else were talking. At one moment the sound of my voice came back to me; I heard those dumb things come pouring out of my mouth and was overcome with a fit of the giggles I couldn't stop; it was awful. It was simply nervousness, spasms you know, contractions coming up out of my belly, I couldn't stop, I was bent over double. I suddenly saw myself playing a role, in fact I really don't know why I'm telling you all this; it's dumb. Like a grand final scene, you know, with the husband who's around fifty, who's bowled over but calm, at the bedside of the consumptive young wife. . . . Sylvie's hand in mine, with him pouring out the usual consolations, with the first silver threads at his temples, imposing and sure of himself, full of restrained grief, as all great grief must be . . . if . . . if . . . when I think back on it, that's what it was, it must have been the contrast that started me giggling. I could suddenly see it all: the gap between the husband whose place I had taken, the husband she would have needed to get out of trouble, and me, who am what I am, eh? no further ahead at twenty-five than I was at twenty or sixteen, with nothing else to do but scrounge around right and left, politely, without minding, just enough to eat, make girls, go to the movies, to Saint Germain . . . to live, that's what, just simply to live and nothing more. And it's already hard for me to get along all by myself—and now with this girl on my hands! You'll tell me that there was more reason to cry than to laugh and that this comparison wasn't very flattering to me. Well, O.k. if you say so. But the fact is that I laughed fit to kill. It was because of being so tired, something must have been triggered the wrong way, something must have gone off the track. . . . Her eyes were fastened on me, fearfully, she was frowning a little as she waited for explanations, but without demanding them, without fuming because I wasn't giving her any. The giggling finally stopped, fortunately. They say it's catching, but she was imperturbable the whole time, or rather, dumfounded.

Then she asked me to tidy her room up for the doctor. I brought her a wet towel and some soap so that she could wash up a little. She was blood-stained all over, and looked like a leper. While she was putting on a clean nightgown, I changed the sheets. And in the middle of all that, I still had to think of asking her for some money to pay the doctor.

"Do you think he's going to notice anything?" she asked me afterward.

"No, why should he? You'll just tell him you fainted. . . . Anyway, what difference does it make? He may even help us."

"Oh, no, not him! Because if he finds out, you see, the whole family will know."

"So?"

"It'd be terrible . . . no, no, it's impossible. . . . Oh, Gilbert, help me!"

I for my part was thinking: "What difference does it make? What matters most is for me not to be involved. Simply a friend she phoned at the last minute."

"Oh, God, if only he doesn't notice anything. . . ."

That's all you heard out of her now. She kept repeating it, she was obsessed, a real animal that had been hunted down. Unless she was dreaming out loud; I don't know.

She jumped when she heard the buzzer. "Damn, there he is," I said to myself, and went to answer the door.

He was a tall, thin guy in a checkered suit, right around fifty, very distinguished, with a black leather bag in his hand. He stood for just a moment on the landing looking at me, puzzled. I was almost afraid that he'd leave again, but he finally came in, offered

me the end of his fingers rather than his hand, and
asked me:

"You're a friend of Sylvie's? I didn't know Sylvie
lived here. . . . "

"Oh, yes, just a friend, that's all. . . . Sylvie called me
after she gashed her forehead just because she was
alone here. . . . "

I must have gotten a little bit mixed up, but he didn't
pursue the subject. He had a long bony face with a
very pointed straight nose and no lips. It must have
been past eleven in the morning, but the hall was dark
and you could hardly see. But just to look at him, I'd
have bet he had bright blue eyes. We went in to Sylvie's bedside. And I noticed by the light of the lamp
that I'd won my bet. But before that . . . I must tell
you . . . I won't forget to my dying day the tone of
voice he used when he said to me, when I tried to show
him the way: "Yes, yes, I've been here before," the
tone of voice in which you say to an interloper, "Well
really, I'm more at home here than you are, am I not?"
And he passed in front of me with one of those side-
long glances. . . . I didn't give a damn. In fact I was
rather glad he was taking over. He certainly wasn't
going to leave this kid in my hands. "You know, Ma-
dame Maresquier's niece has a lover, just imagine, if
only she knew, poor woman! And so young!" That's
what must have been running through his mind, more
or less. Well, might just as well make the best of a bad
job. I fell into step with him, and as I went past the
mirror, I saw for the first time what a state I was in:
really scruffy, my hair not combed, unshaven, my shirt
all wrinkled, dirty. I was unrecognizable. . . . When he

went into Sylvie's room, I thought of modestly disappearing from sight as a mere friend would do, but he called me in without turning around, as if to say: "All right now, none of this play-acting." It was all too plain.

Sylvie smiled at him politely, as white as a sheet. After the customary polite little remarks, he sat down near her, looked at the cut from all angles, and murmured a doctor's mechanical professional words: "Good, good . . . perfect . . . there won't be anything to it." All this time Sylvie was giving me anxious looks behind his back, fr . . . friendly looks, little conspiratorial smiles. I didn't know what in the world to do. I felt like telling her to be a little bit serious. Why not wink at me? Now was certainly the time. He caught on, pushed his chair back, smiled like a bawd at the two of us, and asked me if I was the one who had used handkerchiefs as compresses. It was nice work. And he added:

"Have you been here long?"

"No, half an hour, perhaps, just since Sylvie called me."

He didn't believe me for one second; he obviously thought that I had slept there with her while her aunt was away. He smiled; he looked like he was tickled to death. I had touched his ribald side, that was what counted. Then he sent me into the kitchen to boil the syringe and the needle so as to give her a local anesthetic. When I came back with the pan in my hand, he'd unpacked everything: the alcohol, the cotton, the needles, the thread. He was striding up and down the room, with his thumbs in his vest, a vague, amused smile on his lips. He gave her two injections in her forehead. Sylvie was lying stretched out flat, her eyes half-closed, and she didn't flinch an instant. And yet it must hurt to have injections in your forehead; you hit bone right away.

"There, there was nothing to it, you see," he finally said, or something like it. "You won't feel anything now." His tone of voice was both engaging and distant, but basically much more distant and cold, when I think of it. The sort of guy you never know what tone of voice to use with. A guy who wears an impeccable checkered suit when it's ninety out, with a vest that hangs a bit loosely on him, a stiffly starched collar, a tiepin, and white cuffs without a wrinkle—a guy like that doesn't especially make me feel like sharing secrets with him. Especially the one I had to tell him. Moreover, when it's a subject like that, you have to tread lightly, I think. Doctors have prejudices, personal opinions. There may even be some political question at the bottom of it all, some ethical question, or something like that. I'm not exactly up on such things. . . . I for my part have never had a thing to do with politics. . . . In a word, I had no idea how to bring the subject up . . . the only one that interested Sylvie and me, and for good reason! Sylvie would never dare. He was her family doctor, and I risked making irreparable slips. It's lucky, I said to myself, to have a doctor, a real doctor, on hand, even if he is sort of dumb. He looked more like a racing fan on derby day than a doctor, except that he didn't have binoculars. It was sort of funny to see him lean over Sylvie, who was almost naked, in that outfit of his.

After that, I don't know if you'll be able to understand what happened. . . . It's all a matter of details, of nuances . . . that I do remember, I swear.

He began to look at her, shaking his head. "Something's not right, my dear Sylvie. You're dead white, you look exhausted. A bump on the forehead couldn't have gotten you in such a state. What's the matter?" He repeated the question several times, but as if he were asking himself.

She for her part was smiling as hard as she could so as to reassure him, but nothing came out.

"Come on, tell me what's the matter. Something's wrong, certainly. You looked ghastly when I came in. And this fever of yours isn't from the injections I've given you. . . ."

"It's nothing, nothing, I assure you," Sylvie stammered. "Or rather, I have a slight pain in my liver or it's an attack of indigestion, or something like that, but it's nothing. . . ."

"My word, you look as if you're at death's door, you know," the guy continued with a dreamy look. "I'll have to see what's the matter. . . ."

Sylvie looked at the mantel just then and began to get red as a beet. I looked too. A catastrophe! How could he have not seen it before? I'd left the pan with the syringe and the needle that Claude had used on the mantel between two piles of books. The doctor's was on the night table. There was one too many. I went over and stood in front of the mantel. Too late! The little dry remark came first, in the middle of a deep silence:

"They've been giving you injections? You see? I'm right."

"Yes, Doctor," Sylvie interrupted without budging.

"It's for my liver. It hasn't been going on long though. . . ."

I couldn't get over it. Sylvie had said that in a surprising tone of voice. Relaxed, as if nothing was going on.

He walked over to the mantel, unhurriedly, with his thumbs still in his vest. Unfortunately the box of pills for the hemorrhaging that Claude had brought was still there. I hadn't had time to get it out of sight. When he saw that, he took his thumbs out of his vest, turned on his heels, and came back over to Sylvie's bed. He didn't ask a single question. You'd think he hadn't seen a thing. He took his needle and thread, the cotton and the 90-proof alcohol and concentrated on the gash in her forehead. "There, there, it won't be anything . . ." he kept purring absent-mindedly, as he had before. For the doctor suddenly got very busy, and pressed for time. He wasn't a bit sly or inquisitive now. He did what he had been told to do, period. Maybe his fingers trembled a little. Maybe he was the one who was beginning to be afraid that we'd ask questions or talk to him about something. He was probably thinking: "What kind of a hornets' nest have I gotten myself into?" He obviously had only one thing in mind now: to get out of there. Oh, it really made me laugh, let me tell you! He just asked me for a towel, that was all. Once the stitches were out of the way, he made a bandage with a real compress to show me how it was done, I suppose, put his instruments back into his bag, tapped her hand absent-mindedly, and went to the bathroom to wash his hands. While he was soaping up, I asked him how much I owed him.

"Nothing, nothing," he replied. "We'll take care of that later," he added, getting all absorbed in his washing.

And without waiting for me to see him out, he took his bag and hurried down the hall. I had trouble keeping up with him. He bid me a hasty and rather evasive good-by from a distance as he opened the door without turning around. And before I could even answer him, the silhouette of a racing fan had disappeared down the stairs without waiting for the elevator.

Sylvie was exhausted, drained, squeezed dry like a lemon.

"You've got guts," I told her. "You were great."

The worst of it was that it was true. Sylvie was really a strong girl. Then she told me that I could leave her now, that she wanted to rest, that she was dead tired.

Three hours later, the hemorrhaging had started again, though less badly than before. Her fever had inexplicably gone up even higher. Claude had come back, with red eyes and not in much of a mood to talk. He'd been out for a walk to take the numbness out of his legs and wake up. He gave her another injection. He paced around the apartment like a caged lion, staring into space. He wasn't leaving so as not to leave me in the lurch, not that he didn't feel like doing that, the poor guy. His Sunday was ruined. Sylvie was dozing. All you could hear was a monotonous little sigh that came out of her lips, a sort of rattle that came and went rhythmically in her throat; it was very annoying. She wasn't restless at all now. She just kept moving her head from right to left. She looked at Claude and me without seeing us, with her eyelids half closed, with the eyes of a blind man, you know, when all you can see is the whites of their eyes. There was still that little hissing noise coming out of her mouth, and she wasn't breathing through her nose now; it sounded like a faucet spitting that you wanted to go and shut off once and for all. Moreover, she was burning up.

What Claude couldn't understand was why she should have both hemorrhaging and an infection. That's very rare. Usually blood cleans you out, acts as a disinfectant. He was annoyed that he didn't know why. There was something abnormal about the case that perhaps bothered him, but also made him detached. He seemed more distant, or with his mind far away, if you want to put it that way. Since she was still hemorrhaging, the towels had to be changed because the blood was seeping through and staining the sheets. I was the one who took care of that.

At one moment I opened the window to air the room out. It looked out on a courtyard. A big ray of sunlight came into the room, with the sound of voices, kitchen noises, radios. It was very nice out. The windows were all wide open, but the shutters were closed on account of the heat. That was good, because nobody could catch on to what was going on in this apartment. A housewife with a high-pitched voice was bawling out her kid because he'd forgotten his missal again and was always late for mass. "That's right, it's Sunday," I said. I really felt like going for a walk and not thinking about anything. I dreamed of being on a beach, of going swimming, of going water-skiing, for example, because it's so cool with the water streaming down your legs. But I saw Sylvie moving her head as she looked at me. I realized that the noises and the light were tiring her, and I had to close the window again. Or maybe she found it too sad to watch what was going on outside, the music from the radios, the nice weather, while she was down in bed with a fever. She preferred the room to be dark.

After that, well, after that it got worse still. What can I tell you? There isn't much to tell. Yes . . . Claude gave her still another injection. I began to tell myself it must not be the right injection, or that the penicillin wasn't strong enough, because her fever hadn't gone down; far from it, it was climbing. Sylvie wasn't moving her head any more now, just her lips. She wasn't saying much of anything. There was one sentence that she kept saying over and over again: "I feel I'm going to die, Gilbert . . . I feel I'm going to die . . ."

That may seem silly, but you should have heard the way she kept saying that, in a very low voice, a discreet, humble little voice, not melodramatic at all, as if she were apologizing for not having anything else to say, as if she were begging our pardon. As if we shouldn't be at all surprised; she just wanted to warn us, that's all. So we wouldn't be frightened. You know, like little kids at the table that begin to murmur softly: "I'm going to throw up, I'm going to throw up . . ."—that's how it was. I was at my wits' end, or rather I was dumfounded. It got Claude's goat. "Stop saying such idiotic things," he said to her, "it's absolutely stupid, come on, get hold of yourself, with everything we've given you it'll soon be over." And he walked round and round the bed gesticulating. I was there, kneeling on the edge of the bed, reassuring her, rocking her, telling her to sleep. From time to time I wiped her face with the hand she was not clinging to. Her forehead got covered with sweat in five minutes, and there were tears that must have tickled her cheeks because she grimaced when I didn't sponge her in time with my towel dipped in water. I was in a sort of blue or purple fog, like when you close your eyes, you know; I wasn't conscious of much of anything, it was no use for me to try to keep my eyes open, I felt as if I were having a daydream. And what with the needles and pins in my arms and legs besides, I couldn't feel a thing, I couldn't move. I had lost all notion of time. There was just one gesture that counted for me now: gently wiping her dead-white face, with her eyes damp and panic-stricken, looking at me, calling me, begging me without my knowing exactly why. I had really lost my footing. I wasn't thinking of anything. No, there was one thing I was thinking; I was wondering how the air that she was breathing through her mouth with a noise like a suction pump— she was breathing very loudly, very fast—how this air could be coming out her other hole, down below . . . if there was no connection between the two, you see, between the air she breathed in above and the blood that came out below. It's completely idiotic, but that's really what I was wondering. I almost wished she'd stop breathing to see if the hemorrhaging wouldn't stop at the same time. At one point I wanted to talk to her and I even forgot her name. I looked at her . . . without recognizing her . . . her eyes that slanted a little, her long Venetian blonde hair, her nose that was just a little wide and flat . . . she made me think of a Eurasian, a Vietnamese girl, or something like that, and I yelled:

"Sylvie! Is that you? Wake up, Sylvie!"

"No use yelling at her so loud!" Claude answered.

And it was he who began to yell, calling me an idiot and completely thoughtless. Old Claude was all worked up. I had trouble getting up, it felt as if my legs were dead, they were swollen and I couldn't stand up. He took me over to the other side of the room and said to me—I can still hear him:

"Listen, Gilbert, I can say it now. There's only one thing left to do: take her to the hospital, and right away."

"To the hospital! Are you crazy?" The idea of going to the hospital hit me like a ton of bricks.

"Yes, old man, we've waited too long."

"But she can't be moved," I said. "How do you expect to get her there?"

I didn't have a car. I suggested that we take her in his, but he refused, saying that "as a medical student" he absolutely couldn't be mixed up in anything like this, that it could get him into all sorts of bad trouble. And I know that that was true. I didn't hold it against him at all. But I was running a big risk too, and he knew I was. I could very well find myself being charged with contributing to the delinquency of a minor, and that would have been the living end! They'd already stuck me for a two-months' suspended sentence and four-years' probation, just because I didn't give an idiot girl back her money and on the advice of her family she filed a complaint against me. You'll tell me that swindling

and abortion are two entirely different things. I think so
too, but it's all one and the same to them. Well anyway,
you understand, it was no time to act like an idiot.
What with all the questions, her family on my neck,
and Sylvie who'd end up telling all about it, though I
don't blame her, poor thing, it was one hell of a note.
I really was taking a big risk.

"Are you nuts?" Claude said to me when I'd explained all that to him in great detail. "You can see
what a mess she's in!"

I told him not to talk so loud but a fat lot of good
it did.

"You're completely out of your mind to stay here not
doing a damned thing while she drains herself dry. I'm
not the one who got her knocked up," etc. You can
imagine the sort of arguments.

At one point Sylvie gave a little cry that stopped us
cold. As if she was trying to say something that we
hadn't heard. It was like a cold shower. We both turned
back toward her. We'd been yelling at each other so
loud that she'd heard us. I felt terribly embarrassed. I
had never told her anything about that little sentence I'd
gotten, you see. There wouldn't have been any use in
it. Well, she looked at me and all she did was smile at
me without saying anything, a very pale, very distant
smile; it was very upsetting, now that I think back on it.
She had scarcely moved her lips, and her eyes were
questioning me. She was just waiting for me to make up
my mind about the hospital and tell her. She didn't
hold it against me at all. Her look said: do whatever
you want, don't bother about me. Then when I saw her
watching me with that look in her eyes, I couldn't re-

sist; I felt something cracking, and rushed to the telephone. I looked the number of the municipal hospital
up in the phone book; it wasn't in that part of town,
but Claude said he knew an intern there who might
be on duty.

They answered right away, and asked me what sort
of an emergency it was. I had to answer. I mentioned a
curettage. They didn't ask me any more questions and
told me to get the patient ready. At that moment, I
heard the door slam. It was Claude making the most
of the opportunity. I didn't even have the strength to
run after him.

They were there a quarter of an hour later. Two
guys who didn't say much, with a stretcher, and their
white smocks open over their chests as if they didn't
have anything on underneath. I didn't want to get into
the ambulance. I said that somebody had to notify the
family, that I was only a friend, that she had called me
at the last moment, but for all my saying it several
times, they tossed a blanket to me and I found myself
in the ambulance without knowing how I got there,
sitting next to Sylvie. The ambulance attendant said
very little. At a stop light where there were lots of
people they turned the siren on. It's very impressive.
It's very exciting too. It's like in a movie. Unfortunately
she noticed; that was what I was most afraid of. Then
she looked at me and took my hand. She almost smiled
at me, but she must not have had the strength to. Maybe she found it exciting too, or she was proud to be
hurtling along in an ambulance with the siren on. She
was terribly detached, when you come right down to
it. Everyone in the street saw an ambulance with the

siren going and a shiver went up and down their backs; that happens all the time. But it's not the same thing, I swear to you, to experience it from the inside. There are many fewer people who can say they've experienced that.

I saw the double doors of the entrance open. They brought a stretcher with wheels and put her on it, almost the way you'd clear a buffet table. It was a hard thing to see, I can tell you. There weren't very many people in the courtyard. When they'd taken her away on the stretcher, she had been murmuring: "Gilbert, Gilbert . . ." It was a bother because I didn't want to, or rather I couldn't, give my name, you see, and if I had had to I would have given a false one. In fact, a nurse came with a sort of notebook and asked me if I was one of the family; I said I wasn't and gave the name and address of her parents so that they could notify them, if they hadn't already left on their vacation, that is. I passed myself off as a friend of the family, just to make things easier.

They'd taken Sylvie away to be diagnosed; I couldn't go with her. The nurse told me to sit down in a little yellow room looking out over the courtyard until they came to get me. I had to stay a while, so as to know at least how long she'd be there. I was bushed. I was about to stretch out on the bench so as to sleep a while, when a guy in a white smock came with two others following him.

"You the one that came with the girl, the one who's had an abortion? You're not one of the family, are you?"

"No."

"Why didn't you bring her in earlier?" I recognized

right away by his tone that he was the doctor, the surgeon, and that I shouldn't make any slips.

"I wasn't told right away. And then I didn't know that it was that serious, she didn't want to tell me . . ."

"What a filthy mess!" he interrupted. "It would still have been possible two hours ago."

"Possible to what?"

"To save her."

"Is it that serious, Doctor? You don't mean to tell me . . ."

"Perforation of the uterus, gangrene . . . Curettage won't be much use. Or a transfusion either. We'll do the impossible anyway. . . ."

"It's not all over then?"

"No, not yet. Wait till tomorrow morning. We'll let you know. But don't get your hopes up. She'll die during the night."

I could have burst into tears. I was at the end of my rope. I couldn't believe it. Claude might have warned me though. That was the first time that that had happened to me. Suddenly I had no desire any more to go to sleep. I couldn't imagine Sylvie dying in a hospital bed on a Sunday right in the middle of the summer; no, it was impossible. Had they told her? I thought again of an old green book that I had seen at her aunt's: *The Young Girl's Book of Etiquette*. They must have made her read it at home. There was everything about everything in it: first communion, the first ball and the ones after it, getting engaged, petits fours, and washing one's most intimate parts. I wondered whether there was a chapter on "How to Die in a Hospital." Obviously not. In those days, I suppose, a girl was immortal.

Night was falling. I went out to walk around in the courtyard; the room they'd put me in was becoming really too dreary. Nurses would silently walk by, girls who weren't bad looking at all with their flat heels. Orderlies in espadrilles called to each other as they pushed elderly patients in their wheelchairs; you could see their thin white legs sticking out of their pajamas under the blanket. It felt like warm water was sloshing back and forth in my head. I sat down on a step on top of the stairway in a corner. The balustrade of white stone was all warm from the heat of the day. I was thirsty. I felt dirty and disgusting and wished I could take a shower. I wondered what pal's house I could go to and take one. Because most of my pals are away. And there I was in a hospital courtyard, on the verge of tears! I wondered how long the operation would last. I was tired of waiting. I would have liked to see Sylvie afterward, in her metal bed in a big ward, alone among others. A girl who probably never had set foot in a hospital in her life. Unless they had put her in a room by herself. I dozed. Maybe I even slept, but I would have noticed.

In any case, I recognized him: his long head with no lips, his hurried steps, his checkered suit. He was walking ahead. They were just coming out of the lighted hall through the glass door that opens on the courtyard. Behind him was an old lady, yes, that's what you'd probably call her, a little old lady, with her gray hair pulled severely back into a bun in back, and a handkerchief in her hand, with a very tall, straight distinguished-looking man who was holding her by the arm. They were walking fast. "Well," I said to myself, "I didn't imagine her parents looking that old." They cut diagonally across the courtyard. I was just out of sight, in the north corner of the courtyard. I got up, went back up the stairs, and took the covered walkway to get back to the hall. They had their backs turned to me. I was afraid of only one thing: that the doctor would turn around toward her parents and see me behind them as I made my getaway. I didn't dare look. I felt like running, but people would have looked at me and that would have called their attention to me. I passed through the door looking straight ahead, like an automaton. The two porters in their glass booth at the entrance didn't even raise their heads.

When I found myself out under the chestnut trees in front of the hospital, I took a breath. Even so, there was the police station next door. Then I said to myself: "I've just about had enough of Paris. This city was beginning to get me down. You have to have a change of air, old boy." I was bushed, you see, I felt like a vacation, like seeing the ocean, like relaxing. All I had in my pocket was a thousand-franc bill and my address book. I was ready to leave that very night, if I could find a car that would get me to the coast. To Saint-Tropez or somewhere, there would always be people to get me on my feet again. Meanwhile I had to eat something or I was going to kick off. I rushed across the esplanade and plopped down in the first café-terrace I came across. I ordered two beers in a row with some croissants, and in heat like that, I don't know if you realize it, but I really had to have been hungry, because eating croissants dry, without dunking them in coffee, isn't what I'm fondest of. . . . And when I'd finished, the first idea that came to mind was to call you. I would have done so sooner, believe me. But I hesitated; I thought that you might be a little bit angry with me, you see. . . .

He feels better now. Relieved. Well out of it. He doesn't owe anybody a thing now. It's part of the past. The proof that it's part of the past is that he can tell about it as if it had happened to someone else, as if it were just one story out of a thousand like it. He perhaps hasn't told half of it aloud; he has seen the rest again or heard it, or else it merely passed through his mind. A fresh breeze is coming through the window open on the night. He has stripped to the waist. He has taken off his shoes and the shirt that was beginning to stick to his neck. It's been two days since he changed clothes, not since Saturday, the day the whole thing with Sylvie began. It's unbelievable how fast things go by.

"How old was she?"

He gives a start. She had practically not opened her mouth since the beginning. He had almost forgotten her. Moreover with her, his mistress, no, his faithful pal, it's like a member of the family; what you say isn't important. You're talking for your own benefit. All the time that he was talking she was going back and forth between the bedroom, the kitchen, and the bathroom. But this time she has slammed the door behind her and looks at him, waiting for an answer. He raises his head: she's a rather stocky brunette with short hair, a very delicate nose, and the first signs of wrinkles under her eyes, quite pretty all in all. A little bit older than he is: you'd probably take her to be between twenty-five and thirty.

She has doubtless finished everything she had to do: pick up, do the dinner dishes, take a shower to freshen up. Yes, that's probably it, because she's in a bathrobe, with little drops of water on her face.

"Seventeen. Didn't I tell you that?"

"Yes, you may have at that. . . . Do you want a little rum in your Coke?"

"Yes, that'll pick me up."

The bottle has clinked against his glass; the stream has made a dull, heavy sound. He feels as if he's being born again from out of his fatigue. He spreads his legs, throws his head back in his chair and smiles. A noise, the sound of voices come up from the street: an argument between people on a spree, doubtless. He doesn't even have the strength to go see from the balcony. He doesn't give a damn. Tomorrow his head will be clearer. Tomorrow he can think the whole situation through better. There'll be plenty of time to think of it again, to think of Sylvie. Sylvie who is dying. He can do no more. That's the way things are.

"Do you think we can sleep in this heat?" the woman asks, going over to the bed.

"Not a chance!"

"We can always go to bed meanwhile."

The bed squeaks unpleasantly. "The same old metal springs!" he grumbles. He can't bear beds with metal springs, because of the noise.

"Was it on account of that poor little thing that you dropped me for so long?"

"Me drop you!" he answers in a tired voice. "I never wanted to drop you, old girl, neither this time nor the other times. I thought only of you. You know very well you're the only one that counts; don't give me a hard time."

"And Sylvie?"

"I told you how it happened. . . . She just wasn't lucky. I wasn't either. It's terrible, I know."

She doesn't answer.

"Anyway it's certainly not my fault things turned out that way!" he continues in a violent tone of voice to cut the silence short.

Silence once more.

"Isn't there anything else that can be done?" she finally asks.

"No, the doctors say not."

"And do her parents know your name?"

"No, no . . . nobody does. We always saw each other alone. She talked to me of friends she had, but I never met any of them. I always refused. . . ."

He yawns, passes his hand over his face, rubs his eyes. His skin feels all wrinkled, like an old newspaper.

"You don't look very good, you know," the woman says. "You should go to bed."

"Tomorrow's Monday? Things'll go better, you'll see."

He gets up and undresses with leaden gestures, talking aloud to himself.

"I'll have to pick up my things at my place. I'll get my money and look for another pad before leaving on vacation. . . . In fact, you know, tomorrow I'll also go

look for a job. Something steady, something decent. . . .
I've had enough of being out in the streets. . . ."

"Don't worry. You can stay here as long as you like,
you know that," the woman says.

She has turned out the light.

This time he hasn't heard the metal springs squeak.
The sheets are cool. On the other side of the bed two
little black fires, gentle and patient, await him. She is
lying flat on her belly, her head in her hands, looking
at him in the dark. The two little fires draw closer, then
fall back. Two hands are placed on his back, he feels
himself being drawn closer, he turns over. He'd like so
much to sleep!

"Come on," a warm voice whispers in his ear. "Don't
worry. I know that what happened wasn't your fault.
She was young, she was inexperienced. She was only a
little girl. . . ."

"She was nice though, and pretty, very pretty," he
thinks quickly. "When you come right down to it, I
loved Sylvie." But he says nothing. A question of tact.
Then he says:

"You know, I'd like it very much if I could stay here
a while with you. . . ."

And after a silence: "Basically, it's not as hard as all
that to be happy. I'm stupid to let it get me down."

He took her in his arms then. It took no great effort:
she already had her mouth against his.